# THE FOURTH ORANGE

*BY*

HILLARY DEPIANO

BASED ON *THE MERCHANT* FROM *THE TALE OF TALES* COLLECTION BY GIAMBATTISTA BASILE WITH CHARACTERS FROM CARLO GOZZI'S *THE LOVE OF THREE ORANGES*

## THE TALE OF TALES PROJECT

Giambattista Basile (1566–1632) wrote and compiled the 60 fairy tales within *The Pentamerone* (*Lo cunto de li cunti* in Neapolitan or *The Tale of Tales* in English) in Naples, Italy in the early 1600s. His sister, Adriana, published it in two volumes in 1634 and 1636 after his death. While not widely known, it's important historically because the Brothers Grimm later used it as the source for their far more famous fairy tale collection. *The Tale of Tales* contains the earliest known versions of fairy tales such as Sleeping Beauty, Cinderella, Rapunzel, Puss in Boots, Hansel and Gretel and more.

But I'm not interested in the stories everyone has heard of. I like the obscure ones, the weird ones lost to time. Why do we obsessively retell the same dozen fairy tales when there are plenty of other great ones we ignore?

It bothers me. So, since early 2013, I've been adapting these lesser-known tales for modern audiences to bring these stories back into circulation. I've modernized them with today's audiences in mind while still staying true to the spirit of the originals. Wherever possible, I also preserved the names from the original fairy tale and, where characters were unnamed, I've named them within the historical context and often with names from elsewhere in the Tales themselves.

This project is still ongoing. For the latest list of all the tales I've adapted from The Tale of Tales and what I'm working on next, visit HillaryDePiano.com.

## BIBLIOGRAPHY

Basile, Giambattista (2007). Giambattista Basile's "The Tale of Tales, or Entertainment for Little Ones". Translated by Nancy L. Canepa, illustrated by Carmelo Lettere, foreword by Jack Zipes. Detroit, MI: Wayne State University Press. ISBN 978-0-8143-2866-8.

# STANDALONE ONE-ACTS

There are standalone one-act versions of every fairy tale I've adapted from *The Tale of Tales*.

## *THE MYRTLE*

30-40 minutes, 5 m 8 f (6-20+ performers possible)
A prince discovers his myrtle tree turns into a fairy maiden at sundown.

## *GOOSED!*

(based on *The Goose*)
25-35 minutes, 2 m 6 f 8 any (11-20+ performers possible)
Two poor sisters rescue a golden goose but their sneaky neighbors want it for themselves.

## *ARM CANDY*

(based on *Pintosmalto)*
35-45 minutes, 2 m, 4 f (5-7+ performers possible)
When a brilliant inventor builds the perfect husband out of sugar, he's stolen by a queen who wants him for herself.

## *THE FOURTH ORANGE*

(based on *The Merchant* with characters from Carlo Gozzi's *The Love of Three Oranges*)
20-30 minutes, 4 m, 6 f, 5 any (7-20+ actors possible)
There were only supposed to be three oranges but Franceschina had to stick her nose where it didn't belong.

## *THE SHE BEAR*

25-35 minutes, 2 m 2 f (4-10+ performers possible)
Is the prince losing his mind or has he really fallen in love with a bear?

## *VARDIELLO*

10-15 minutes, 1 m, 1 f, 2 any
How much damage can one half-wit do before his mother gives him

the boot?

**Want to combine plays to make an evening's entertainment?**
You'll find shortened versions of the most popular fairy tales in this
fun and fantastical full length!

# *THE FOURTH ORANGE*

### *AND OTHER FAIRY TALES YOU'VE NEVER EVEN HEARD OF*

100-120 minutes, 25w 12m 11any (11 to 60+ performers possible)
It's bedtime bedlam when a washed-up clown tries to sell three unruly
princesses on something other than their fairy tale favorites.

**Looking for something even more flexible?**
Mix and match the tales above to create an evening's entertainment
and I'll provide interstitial material and opening and closing scenes to
connect the tales together no matter what combination you choose!

For more information about this custom option, email Hillary
DePiano.

*Photos by Scot Whitman, Rutgers Prep, November 2017*

# THE FOURTH ORANGE

**The Fourth Orange** premiered on November 16-18, 2017 at Rutgers Preparatory School in Somerset, NJ with the following cast and crew.

| | |
|---|---|
| TRUFFALDINO | Nate Lyles |
| FRANCESCHINA | Skyllar Capuno |
| CREONTA | Aarushi Roperia |
| PRINCESS NINETTA | Tabetha Kiraz |
| PRINCESS LINETTA | Emma Sperr |
| PRINCESS NICOLETTA | Livia Lee |
| PRINCE TARTAGLIA | Daniel Forte |
| THE GRIEVING GHOST | Kevin Tao |
| BANDITS | Rocky Meng |
| | Sachin Mathew |
| THE SEXIEST GUY EVER | Qingshi Meng |
| RANDOM PEASANT | Dan Jenkins |
| PRINCESS MENECHELLA | Téa Guarino |

## ENSEMBLE

Selena Adrianzen, Samantha Barbato, Daria Bresnick, Emmett Duffy, Carla Evans, Kaylah Holmes, Esha Mehta, Christal Onyekwere, Elaine Rodriguez, Paris Townsell, LongGe (Andrea) Wang, Richard Xiang

| | |
|---|---|
| Directed by | Cora M. Turlish |
| Assistant Directed by | Manuela Curutchet Stevenson |
| Student Assistant Director | Tara Viswanath |
| Set Design by | Erin Drakoulis |
| Set Construction Coordination by | Derrick Laurion |
| Lighting Design & Direction by | Michael Nardulli |
| Costumes by | Christina Kratzman |
| Stage Managed by | Sunny Chen |
| Assistant Stage Manager | Aela Williams |
| Lighting Board Operator | Jamie Chen |
| Sound Board Operator | Michael Slass |
| Backstage Crew | David Chen, Jonina Yang |
| Publicity Art | Skyllar Capuno |
| Make Up Coordinator | Kuntal Thakkar |

### Set Construction
David Chen, Jamie Chen, Jesse Cross, Liz Gambacorta, Zac Gambacorta, Libby Gilfeather, Nya Johnson, Val Lazarczyk, Matthew Romage, Rishie Seshadri, Michael Slass, Emma Sperr, Jonina Yang

### Make-up
Aaditi Ahlawat, Amrin Ashraf, Mahima Chaluvadi, Rachel Emmett, Isabelle Fehl, Nithya Goel, Lauren Hanna, Catherine Harbour, Ava Margolis, Eloise Meek, Kuntal Thakkar, Tara Viswanath

~

The playwright extends her greatest heartfelt thanks to the following groups who workshopped early versions of this play. It is thanks to your excellent cast and crews that this show is what it is today!

# SIERRA HIGH SCHOOL
JANUARY 11-20TH, 2017

# RUTGERS PREPARATORY SCHOOL
NOVEMBER 16-18TH, 2017

# PRODUCTION NOTES

## IMPROVISATION

In the spirit of the slapstick of classic Italian theatre and commedia dell'arte tradition that inspired these adaptations, you're encouraged to put your own spin on all comedic bits and fights and to explore the physical comedy through improvisation. If you can come up with something funnier than the stage directions describe, go for it! I'm even happy to approve changes in dialog or more modern references, just run it by me first. For performer safety, avoid injury by always making sure you finalize all physical routines before the show opens. While you certainly don't have to, you're welcome to perform the show in masked commedia style if desired.

## CONTENT

While this fairy tale is PG as written (as most classic fairy tales are), I'm happy to work with schools and other groups who may need to tone it down to be able to perform it. Be it language or situational, please email me (hillary@hillarydepiano.com) with any issues you run into. I'll do my best to help you find a workaround.

## CASTING NOTES

I encourage blind casting in all cases where it comes to race, gender, body type, etc. If you're in a casting pickle, please email me to explain your casting needs and I'll help you out. I can give you alternate character names and lines or grant permission to change character genders as needed, whatever we need to do to make it happen.

## STAGING

Staging for this play can be as simple or as complicated as you want it to be. Because of the storybook nature of the tales, costumes can be anything from elaborate period pieces to paper bag tunics with just a few elements to suggest the character. Sets can be elaborately illustrated pages from a picture book, the crayon drawings of a child's imagination or a few furniture pieces where the audience's imagination does the rest.

## INCREASING OR DECREASING CAST SIZE

Need more roles? Young Truffaldino can be a different performer than Old Truffaldino. I've also only specified one grieving ghost, though the original tale has three total. Random Peasant can be a single spokesperson for the crowd or you may divide those lines up between multiple ensemble members.

Sparky can be a large puppet manipulated by one performer or several. Alternately, a separate performer can play each head with a long material "neck" that stretches behind and attaches to a stationary body. While the dragon has seven heads in the original fairy tale, you are welcome to reduce this number to three if it makes it easier.

**Please don't hesitate to contact me (hillary@hillarydepiano.com) for any reason. I'm here to help!**

# CHARACTERS
### (In order of appearance)

TRUFFALDINO, a once famous clown
FRANCESCHINA, butcher girl, delivers sausages
CREONTA, fearsome evil witch, loyal customer
PRINCESS NINETTA, princess captured by Creonta
PRINCESS LINETTA, Princess Ninetta's sister
PRINCESS NICOLETTA, Princess Ninetta's other sister
PRINCE TARTAGLIA, lover of three oranges
THE GRIEVING GHOST, deceased purveyor of ghost nonsense
FAIRY PRINCE, currently being kidnapped
BANDITS, doing the kidnapping
THE SEXIEST GUY EVER, sexy guy with scary magic hair
RANDOM PEASANT, hapless bystander(s)
PRINCESS MENECHELLA, princess being fed to dragon
SPARKY, dragon with seven regenerating heads

**SETTING**
A fairytale kingdom.

**TIME**
The imaginary past.

## THE FOURTH ORANGE
## SCENE 1

*(Truffaldino leaps onto the stage expectantly.)*

### TRUFFALDINO

Ta dah! I'm here! Well, what are you waiting for? Don't you people know you're in the presence of the famous clown, Truffaldino? Jester to important kings, squire to heroic princes, star of many a funny fairy tale! No? Nothing? Can someone at least give me a little "woo" or something?

*(if no one immediately does)*
Man, tough crowd.  Come on, now. I'm not getting things started until I get at least one "wooo!"

*(he cajoles them, maybe even singles someone out until he gets a "woo")*
Thank you! Anyone who's willing to make a fool of themselves is my kind of person. The rest of you were ready to leave me hanging up here. You were all just sitting there waiting for somebody to do it, completely forgetting that you're somebody. Which reminds me of a story. There were only supposed to be three oranges. That's the fairy tale everybody knows, right? The Three Oranges, though not every version highlights my own heroic role in that adventure to my liking. Three oranges, three ladies trapped inside, some fella saves them, blah blah happily ever after, right? Except that's not the whole story. It's time somebody told you about The Fourth Orange and I'm just the clown for the job because I was there. Hold onto your butts, folks, because Truffaldino is narrating this one so you know it's going get wacky.

*(The stage is set for a creepy courtyard outside Creonta's castle.)*

### TRUFFALDINO

Aw yeah, we've got scenery and stuff now. Let's do this! So, once upon a time, a peasant girl came to the castle of the fearsome witch Creonta on a simple errand.

*(Franceschina enters with a basket. She knocks
tentatively on the rusted gate.)*

## FRANCESCHINA

Hello? Creonta, your witch...liness? It's me, the butcher's daughter,
with your order of... Is anyone here?

*(She goes to knock again but, before she can touch the
gate, it swings open with a long eerie squeal. A scream
comes from the castle but is quickly muffled.)*

OK. So it's super creepy here. At least it's not boring like back at the
shop. Besides, she's a witch, creepy's her thing. I don't understand why
my parents have to be so hexist about it.

*(With a crash of thunder, the fearsome hag, Creonta,
appears from nowhere. Franceschina screams. Creonta
cackles.)*

## CREONTA

Got you good that time, didn't I?

## FRANCESCHINA

Yeah, you did! That was awesome. My heart nearly stopped beating!

## CREONTA

Nearly? Must be losing my touch. We'll go for a full skipped beat next
time.

## FRANCESCHINA

Oh. Well, about that. I'm afraid this is the last delivery.

## CREONTA

Nonsense.

## FRANCESCHINA

I'm really sorry. My folks were furious when they found out I was
coming here. They're just so paranoid about getting mixed up in all
this fairy tale stuff. They think I'm going to get turned to stone or
cursed to fall in love with a singing apple or something. As if anything
that interesting ever happens to me!

## CREONTA

But where will I get Sparky her sausages? No one makes them like you do. My little baby loves them so, don't you, girl?

*(A roar from offstage.)*

## FRANCESCHINA

That's a little baby?

## CREONTA

Barely a hatchling! Hasn't even grown half her heads yet and still doesn't have the sense not to gobble up her favorites without chewing. She'd choke on those sausages if I didn't cut them up nice--

*(A crash offstage. Creonta freezes, sniffing the air.)*
Aha! Freed yourselves from my little cage, did you? Never mind, pretties. Creonta loves a chase!

*(Creonta disappears as suddenly as she came.)*

## FRANCESCHINA

Wait! You forgot your... I guess I'll just leave this by the front door so she'll-- Oof!

*(She heads towards the castle only to collide with the three frantic princesses who burst out the door. They end up in a heap, the princesses scrambling to right themselves.)*

## PRINCESS LINETTA

No! Please, we must get away!

## PRINCESS NICOLETTA

The witch is nearly upon us!

## PRINCESS NINETTA

The gate is open! If we can only reach it in time!

## FRANCESCHINA

Whoa! Honest-to-goodness damsels in distress!

*(The princesses get to their feet and run towards the*

*gate but, just as they get there, it slams shut. They
pound and pull but it won't budge. With a flash,
Creonta returns to the courtyard.)*

### CREONTA

Surely my little doves didn't think they could fly away that easily?

### PRINCESS NINETTA

Please, our father is King of Antipodes. Whatever you desire, he'll grant it.

### CREONTA

I know who your father is and he has crossed me for the last time. Now that his precious dolls are mine, I'll have my revenge at last.

### PRINCESS LINETTA

No! We beg of you, have mercy!

### PRINCESS NICOLETTA

Surely there is some brave hero who will come to our rescue?

*(Creonta cackles and conjures a large knife.)*

### CREONTA

No one's coming, child. You're all alone.

*(Franceschina clears her throat.)*
Don't be a fool, Franceschina. This affair is none of your concern.

### FRANCESCHINA

Well, it's got to be somebody's and there's nobody else here.

### CREONTA

You must be joking. What could you possibly do against all this power?

### FRANCESCHINA

I could ask you nicely to please not hurt them?

### CREONTA

Very well, I won't hurt them.

*(Her knife becomes a magic wand.)*
I'll keep them for my collection. These three should transform beautifully into flowers or maybe even some fruit. Yes, lovely fresh fruit. A pretty prison of enchantment.

PRINCESS NICOLETTA
No! We'll be frozen in time!

PRINCESS LINETTA
Trapped forever! It's a fate worse than death!

PRINCESS NINETTA
What have you done? You've doomed us!

FRANCESCHINA
I didn't know, I take it back, I--

CREONTA
Some hero. We all have our roles to play and you'd do best to mind yours before you make things any worse.

*(She lifts her wand. The princesses cower.
Franceschina runs between them.)*

FRANCESCHINA
Wait! Stop! You can't just turn people into fruit!

CREONTA
Can't I? Watch me.

TRUFFALDINO
And before the butcher girl could speak again, the witch raised her wand and, with a blast of her magic, poof! She was an orange.

*(Creonta raises her wand and zaps Franceschina.
Franceschina screams and turns into an orange.)*

CREONTA
Silly girl. You should have stuck to sausages.

*(Creonta turns to the princesses.)*

PRINCESS NINETTA

No!

PRINCESS LINETTA

Stop!

PRINCESS NICOLETTA

Please...

CREONTA

Enough.

*(The princesses scream as Creonta turns them into oranges too. Their three oranges are huddled together while Franceschina's orange stands apart.)*

TRUFFALDINO

When the smoke cleared, the princesses were gone and three more oranges stood in their place.

CREONTA

Well, Franceschina, orange you glad you stuck your nose where it didn't belong? You thought you were bored before? Now you've got all of eternity to wish you'd minded your business. Ha!

*(She goes back to her castle.)*

## SCENE 2

TRUFFALDINO

And that was that. The witch continued her wicked ways but the peasant and the princesses could only watch as the world aged around them.

*(Many years pass. While the princesses' oranges remain pristine, branches and other random debris fall onto Franceschina's orange, partially obscuring it.)*

The days collected up into months which piled up to make years and a big fat nothing changed for the prisoners of the peel. Until, one day, a prince and his dashingly handsome squire battled their way into Creonta's courtyard.

*(Prince Tartaglia, his armor improvised from pots and pans, bashes through the gate and makes his way to the three oranges.)*

## TARTAGLIA

I'm coming, my dearest oranges! There they are!

## TRUFFALDINO

But, unfortunately for our heroine, the prince only had love for three oranges.

## TARTAGLIA

Squire? A little help?

## TRUFFALDINO

Oh! That's me.

*(Truffaldino assumes the role of his younger self, Tartaglia's squire.)*
Coming, your highness!

## FRANCESCHINA

*(muffled, from within orange)* Hey! What about me?

*(They don't hear her. Truffaldino helps Tartaglia collect the three oranges and they exit pursued by Creonta.)*

## CREONTA

No! He's taken them! My oranges! My precious oranges!

*(She runs off after them. Lightning streaks across the sky. Creonta screams. Truffaldino pops back in to narrate.)*

## TRUFFALDINO

As the prince and I took the three oranges away for their happy ever after, lightning flashed and the witch let out a terrible scream. Then there was nothing. Soon the only evidence of Creonta's evil reign was a single orange in a ruined courtyard, alone and forgotten. A bit of collateral damage from someone else's fairy tale. But, in time, the magic that bound the orange grew weaker and weaker until...

> *(Franceschina's orange rocks for a moment until she manages to force a fist through the skin. She battles her way out, kicking her way free of both peel and the debris that's collected on top of it over the years.)*

### FRANCESCHINA

Finally! Free! I have such a new respect for baby birds. Whoa, what happened here? Where is everybody?

### TRUFFALDINO

As she picked through what was left of the castle, she realized decades had passed while she'd been trapped in the orange.

### FRANCESCHINA

Everything... everyone I knew. They're all long gone.

### TRUFFALDINO

Everything, that is, but...

> *(Franceschina finds the basket in the remains of her orange.)*

### FRANCESCHINA

The basket. Of course. None of this would have happened if I'd only... Fine. Lesson learned. From now on, I stick to delivering sausages. Now, where is that witch?

> *(She grabs her basket and exits)*

## SCENE 3

### TRUFFALDINO

There was a trail of wreckage leading from the ruins and the girl followed it for weeks.

### FRANCESCHINA

All I have to do is deliver this last order of sausages and my life will be back on track. And I'm not getting sucked into anymore fairy tale trouble, that's for sure.

TRUFFALDINO

But that was harder than she thought. On the first night of her journey, she sheltered in an old barn that turned out to be haunted by a grieving ghost that would not be ignored.

*(A ghost appears before Franceschina making spooky sounds that resolve into exaggerated sobbing. She tries to ignore it but it gets up in her face.)*

THE GRIEVING GHOST

Boo! Hoo-hoo... Boo-hoo-hoo... Booooo-hoooooo-hoooooo...

FRANCESCHINA

Oh, fine. Uh, don't cry. There there. It'll be OK.

TRUFFALDINO

The spirit was so grateful for her sympathy, it presented her with its hidden treasure.

*(Ghost hands her a chest.)*

FRANCESCHINA

What's this? Whoa. There's like a fortune in gold coins here. Wait. Let me guess, they're stolen or cursed or magic or some other ghost nonsense, right?

*(Ghost dances around mysteriously)*

THE GRIEVING GHOST

OoooooooOOOOOOooooooooOOOOOooooooooOOOOOOOooooooo--

FRANCESCHINA

OK, stop it.

THE GRIEVING GHOST

Boo.

*(Crestfallen, the ghost exits.)*

TRUFFALDINO

But the girl didn't want to deal with any ghost nonsense so she quickly foisted the treasure off on the first person she saw.

*(Bandits enter carrying a wrapped parcel that wiggles and mumbles suspiciously. Franceschina hands one the gold.)*

FRANCESCHINA

Here, buddy, free treasure. Have fun with it.

BANDIT

What's this? Gold! A whole mess of it! We're rich!

BANDIT 2

Now we don't even need to bother torturing fancy pants here for the fairy treasure, we got our own! Woohoo!

*(They drop their parcel, which emits a muffled "ow", and run off celebrating.)*

FRANCESCHINA

There. All done with that. Now to get back on my way.

TRUFFALDINO

She had managed to get rid of the gold alright but, in doing so, she'd accidentally saved a fairy prince from certain death at the hand of bloodthirsty bandits.

FRANCESCHINA

Shut up, I did not.

*(A fairy emerges from the parcel)*

FAIRY PRINCE

Dearest maiden, you have saved me from a terrible fate!

FRANCESCHINA

Salty ham hocks, seriously?

TRUFFALDINO

Seriously. The prince invited her back to the fairy kingdom where...

FAIRY PRINCE

I will grant you wishes beyond your imagining.

TRUFFALDINO

Which was a pretty sweet deal. But still she refused.

FRANCESCHINA

You know, I'd really love to but... I have to pass... because I've got this thing with these sausages. So... bye.

*(She continues on.)*

TRUFFALDINO

Yes, no temptation could make her stray from her path. Not even when she left the prince and came upon the sexiest dude ever leaning against the door of his palace with his shirt all open and his manly man hair flowing and his eyes doing the sexy eye stuff and everything.

*(Sexy music as The Sexiest Dude Ever comes into view. A breeze blows open his silk shirt and tosses his impressive locks and as he leans seductively against the doorway of his palace. Think vintage romance novel cover model. Franceschina tries to ignore him.)*

THE SEXIEST DUDE EVER

Hello there, m'lady. Won't you rest a moment and partake of the pleasures of my palace?

FRANCESCHINA

La la la, I don't hear anything...

TRUFFALDINO

Even him, she ignored which actually turned out to be for the best because he would have tried to imprison her forever suspended in a web of magic hair that you can only escape with an enchanted dog that can unhinge its jaw to swallow him whole so, honestly, a good call on skipping that one.

FRANCESCHINA

I'm sorry, what? Magic hair?

THE SEXIEST DUDE EVER

Like this! Hair of mine, bind her! You will be mine!

*(He goes all evil and his hair reaches out like tentacles to bind her.)*

FRANCESCHINA

What the holy hairy whaaaaaaaah!

*(Franceschina fights off the fierce follicles and hurries offstage. All exit.)*

SCENE 4

*(A castle courtyard draped in mourning. A harried Franceschina rushes in.)*

TRUFFALDINO

So it went until one day, the trail ended in a strange kingdom all draped in mourning.

*(She stops a random peasant hurrying past. Random Peasant can be several people with lines divided between them.)*

FRANCESCHINA

Hey! You! Random peasant!

RANDOM PEASANT

Me? But--

FRANCESCHINA

No. I don't want to hear it, OK? I don't care about your talking cat or your giant flea or your brother in law who's a dolphin or whatever fairy tale weirdness you're just dying to drag me into. I am staying out of it. I've got one job and that's finding Creonta so I can finally deliver this basket of sausages.

RANDOM PEASANT

Creonta? The old witch? But she's long dead.

FRANCESCHINA

She's dead? But then how can I--

*(Royal guards drag Princess Menechella in kicking and*

*screaming. They chain her to a blood-stained boulder in the center of the castle courtyard. Bones, armor and weapons from previous victims are strew about it.)*

## MENECHELLA

Let go of me! I don't care if my name came up, the King's daughter shouldn't even be in the drawing in the first place. It's not going to appreciate my royal blood. You might as well just feed it another worthless peasant. Stop this right now!

## FRANCESCHINA

What's going on over-- Wait. It's not more fairy tale stuff, is it?

## RANDOM PEASANT

No, no. It's nothing like that. They're just feeding the princess to the enchanted dragon who must get a daily sacrifice or it will destroy the entire kingdom.

## FRANCESCHINA

How do I keep walking into these situations? Is there a sign on my back or something?

*(The guards finish securing the princess. They exit.)*

## MENECHELLA

No! What are you doing? Don't leave me! I command you to come back here right this instant and untie me! Oh, thank the gods! They're coming back! I knew my father would come to his senses.

*(Guards enter dragging young Truffaldino who they chain up next to her)*

## TRUFFALDINO

Now hold on a minute here, fellas. Can't we talk about this?

## MENECHELLA

Yes. Much better. Feed it the jester. Nobody will miss him anyway.

## TRUFFALDINO

Hey! I'll miss me!

*(Once he's secured, the guards leave)*

MENECHELLA
Wait! You can't go! You haven't released me. No!

TRUFFALDINO
Princess Menechella. Fancy meeting you here.

MENECHELLA
Shut up, Truffaldino. It's not fair. I did everything I was supposed to. All the stupid prim and proper princess stuff. Years of bows and balls and blah. And for what?

TRUFFALDINO
You? What about me? All I did was tell one, very tasteful, joke about the size of the King's codpiece and--

MENECHELLA
You dunce.

TRUFFALDINO
I'm a clown! What do you expect? I was trying to get him to end my contract. I didn't think he'd end me!

*(A terrible roar. Menechella and Truffaldino shriek and clutch each other.)*

MENECHELLA
No! I'm too pretty to die!

TRUFFALDINO
Me too!

FRANCESCHINA
It eats one of you every day?

RANDOM PEASANT
Two on cheat days.

*(Another roar.)*

FRANCESCHINA

Why doesn't someone do something?

RANDOM PEASANT
You know how it is, miss, you've got those sausages. Us, we're bystanders. We stand. By. Like this.

*(Peasants begin standing by)*

FRANCESCHINA
But you'll eventually all be eaten either way, you might as well... Hello? Hey, don't go all ensemble on me, I'm--

*(Two roars at once.)*
This is ridiculous! You all played your part to the letter and you're still up to your eyeballs in trouble. It's not like the dragon's all that concerned about shoving its muzzle into someone else's business.

*(She wrests an old ax from a skeleton's hand and starts to chop at the chains)*

MENECHELLA
Watch it! What are you doing?

FRANCESCHINA
Something. Someone's got to. Hold still!

MENECHELLA
You don't look much like a hero.

TRUFFALDINO
She looks like she's saving our butts. Pretty sure that's the only requirement. But, uh, maybe hurry it up a bit?

FRANCESCHINA
I'm trying! These chains are really thick!

*(A chorus of roars. Heavy footsteps approach.)*
Oh, bratwurst. I don't suppose it's, like, a small dragon, is it?

TRUFFALDINO
It's huge!

FRANCESCHINA

Of course it is.

MENECHELLA

It's a horrible creature with the wings of a bat and eyes of fire! It's got this huge mouth filled with the sharp teeth of a Corsican hound where every fang drips with acidic drool.

FRANCESCHINA

*(awed)* That sounds...

TRUFFALDINO

Yeah and it's got the mewing face of a giant cat with a comb on top like a rooster and the paws of a bear with a tail shaped like a big snake!

FRANCESCHINA

*(no longer awed)* ...pretty silly, actually. I can't even picture that.

MENECHELLA

You don't need to picture it. It's here!
    *(She screams as a dragon head comes into view.)*

FRANCESCHINA

Wow. It really is goofy looking.

    *(Dragon roars.)*
Aah! No offense! Whoa!

    *(The dragon lunges for her. A brief battle. After a few
    close calls, she manages to chop off its head.)*
Ha! I did it! I slay the dragon! I wasn't even planning to, I just said to myself, self, it's no different than the block behind the butcher shop back home but with a really really big chicken and I swung and--

    *(A chorus of angry roars)*
There's more than one?

TRUFFALDINO

Not exactly.

*(The rest of the dragon enters. It has seven heads total.)*

### FRANCESCHINA

You went on and on about acid drool and eyes like fire and you didn't think the fact that it's got seven heads worth mentioning?

### MENECHELLA

What kind of half rate dragon do you think my father would feed me to?

### TRUFFALDINO

And that's not all. See?

*(The other heads are reattaching the severed head)*

### FRANCESCHINA

Seven regenerating heads. Again, something you'd think would make the list of highlights.

*(Her ax finally breaks the chains.)*

### MENECHELLA

Finally! I'm out of here.

### FRANCESCHINA

Good plan.

### TRUFFALDINO

Screaming and running for my life happen to be specialties of mine.

*(Menechella tosses her chains back over Franceschina and Truffaldino. They struggle to untangle themselves)*

### MENECHELLA

Um, no. You two aren't going anywhere. It has to eat somebody or it'll destroy the whole kingdom. So you're up, unless you want to feed it one of them.

*(Bystanders stand by harder)*

### FRANCESCHINA

What?

TRUFFALDINO

Why you...

MENECHELLA

Loyal subjects, the kingdom will be forever grateful for your brave
sacrifice and every year I will light a candle and mourn you for your
selfless, blah blah blah, whatever. Later, suckers!

*(She runs away. All seven heads roar at once and
advance on Franceschina and Truffaldino.)*

TRUFFALDINO

Nice dragon...

FRANCESCHINA

Ah ha ha. I hope you're not taking that whole decapitation thing
personally. Just a little joke, you know, amongst friends and you've got
it back on now so every thing's alright and... Aaaah!

*(The dragon goes for them. Franceschina and
Truffaldino run around screaming wildly, dodging
snapping heads, until the dragon's neck is tied in knots.
It wails and struggles to untie itself. They hide and
catch their breath.)*
Huh. That worked out better than expected.

TRUFFALDINO

Well, it's already untangling itself so now seems like an excellent time
to run for our lives and never look back.

FRANCESCHINA

Wait. Princess Menechella's right. If it doesn't eat someone, it'll
destroy the whole kingdom.

TRUFFALDINO

I'm not a man of much moral center but I'm going to take a stab here
and say... that's bad and something I totally care about?

*(The dragon has untangled itself. Unable to find
Franceschina and Truffaldino, it starts to destroy the
town. Smoke, fire and chaos. Bystanders scream,*

*scatter and get eaten.)*

RANDOM PEASANT

Aaah! Help! Help! It's got me! Noooo!

FRANCESCHINA

Oh, no no. Fatty pork butt, I did it again. I made it worse. Now this whole place is going to be charred rubble and it's all my fault. I should have stuck to sausages. These completely useless sausages.

*(She throws her basket of sausages at the dragon. The dragon stops tug of war-ing a random peasant between two of its mouths and turns towards the sausages. After an experimental sniff, the heads begin to gather around the basket, eating voraciously.)*

TRUFFALDINO

Hey! You found something it loves to eat more than people! Look at it gobble those sausages up. It's barely taking time to chew.

FRANCESCHINA

Gobbling them up... Sparky? I can't believe it. Sparky, is that you?

*(The dragon starts to choke)*
Wait a minute, not so fast, those aren't cut up small enough, you'll...

*(At once, all heads freeze and then collapse, dead)*
...choke.

*(Truffaldino gives the dragon an experimental kick)*

TRUFFALDINO

Huh. It's dead.

*(All the peasants cheer and celebrate.)*

RANDOM PEASANT

The dragon's dead! We're saved! Yay! Huzzah! Yayzzah!

FRANCESCHINA

Oh, Sparky. You know, those sausages were for her in the first place. I completed my delivery after all.

TRUFFALDINO

Wow. Just goes to show... something, probably.

FRANCESCHINA

Yup.

RANDOM PEASANT

The dragon has been slain by a true hero at last! As the king decreed,
"Whoever should slay the dragon shall be awarded half the kingdom
and wed the princess herself."

FRANCESCHINA

I'm not--

RANDOM PEASANT

Oh, it's fine. We're a very progressive kingdom.

FRANCESCHINA

No, I mean, I'm not interested in ruling a kingdom or wedding royalty
or anything that sounds like a boring happily ever after just yet. From
now on, I'm choosing my own path and seeing what adventures it leads
to.

TRUFFALDINO

That's the spirit! And, in my experience, all the best paths lead down to
the tavern. I am downright parched after all that excitement. Seeing as
you saved me from certain death and all, I suppose I owe you a round.
I'm Truffaldino, by the way.

FRANCESCHINA

Franceschina.

TRUFFALDINO

Well, Franny, what do you say?

RANDOM PEASANT

But the King's decree...

FRANCESCHINA

Tell you what. You claim it. Anyone asks, you slew the dragon.
Maybe cut off its tongues or something, bring them to the King. Kings

like stuff like that.

RANDOM PEASANT
Me? Ruler of the land? Wed to the princess?

FRANCESCHINA
Sure. Why not?

RANDOM PEASANT
I go to claim my destiny!

*(Runs off)*

TRUFFALDINO
Was that a good idea?

FRANCESCHINA
Sure. Everyone deserves a chance to be the hero.

*(As they leave)*

TRUFFALDINO
You know, I've done some pretty heroic things myself.

FRANCESCHINA
That so?

TRUFFALDINO
Oh yeah. You ever hear the story of the three oranges?

FRANCESCHINA
Heard it? I was the fourth orange. The one that prince and his fool of a squire left behind to rot when they rescued the other three. What about it?

TRUFFALDINO
Uh, nothing. Nothing whatsoever.

*(They exit. Truffaldino comes back out as narrator and says)*
And so they lived happily ever--

*(Franceschina rushes back out)*

## FRANCESCHINA

Whoa, hey, Truff, not yet! Don't you dare narrate me off into the sunset! I'm only just getting started.

## TRUFFALDINO

Well, yeah, I know but this particular story is done and I gotta end it somehow.

## FRANCESCHINA

Then how about this. Folks, don't spend so much time worrying about staying in your lane that you miss your exit. You're the main character of your story. So, go on, get out there in the part you want to be playing, not just the one that was handed to you. Good enough?

## TRUFFALDINO

Yeah. Nice work. Motivational even. I hit me right here in the-- hmm, wait, no that was just gas.

## FRANCESCHINA

And you're ruining it.

## TRUFFALDINO

So, the tavern. Shall we, m'lady?

## FRANCESCHINA

We shall, you big goof. Goodnight everybody! May you all live happily ever after... that is, when you want to. If you want to. And how you want to! Yeah. Bye.

*(Exit)*

# ALSO BY HILLARY DEPIANO

HILLARYDEPIANO.COM

## FULL LENGTH PLAYS

### *THE LOVE OF THREE ORANGES*
comedy / fantasy /commedia dell'arte
90 to 120 minutes, 8 f, 8 m, 5 any (13-40+ actors possible: 7-20 f, 5-20 m)
*A prince is cursed to fall in love with three magical oranges.*

### *THE GREEN BIRD*
comedy / fantasy /commedia dell'arte
90 to 120 minutes, 4 m 6 f 3 any (13-40+ actors possible)
*Four royals, two clowns, and way too many talking statues must unravel the mystery of the green bird before an evil queen destroys the kingdom.*

## ONE ACT PLAYS

### *DADDY ISSUES*
drama
15 to 20 minutes, 1 female, 1 male, 3 any
*A young woman must confront the ghost of her past.*

### *POLAR TWILIGHT*
comedy / holiday
20 to 25 minutes, 3 f, 3 m (6 actors possible: 0-5 f, 1-6 m)
*Everything you know about Santa is wrong and the truth kind of... sucks. Vampire Santa Claus... but in a cute way!*

### *NEW YEAR'S THIEVE*
comedy / holiday
30 to 35 minutes, 2 m 3 f 3 any (7 to 10+ actors possible)
*Someone's stolen the New Year and the main suspect is... Frosty the coat rack?*

### *WEAK DAYS*
comedy
45 to 60 minutes, 6-7 any
*All five weekdays play out at simultaneously across the stage in a comic ballet. Winner of The Chameleon Theatre Circle's 16th Annual New Play Contest.*

### *THE LOVE OF THREE ORANGES (ONE ACT VERSION)*
comedy / fantasy /commedia dell'arte
35 to 40 minutes, 8 f, 6 m, 4 any (10-30+ actors possible)
*A prince is cursed to fall in love with three magical oranges.*

### *THE GREEN BIRD (ONE ACT VERSION)*
comedy / fantasy /commedia dell'arte
35 to 45 minutes, 4 m 6 f 3 any (12-40+ actors possible)

*Four royals, two clowns, and way too many talking statues must unravel the mystery of the green bird before an evil queen destroys the kingdom.*

# SHORT PLAYS (10-15 MINUTES)
*THE RAVEN / LENORE*
*THE THREE LITTLE PIGS AND THE BIG BAD STORM*
*THE (COMPLETELY INACCURATE) LEGEND OF THE MUMMY WITCH HOUSE*
*MASKS*
*THE COMPLETE NOVELS OF JANE AUSTEN: NOW NEW AND IMPROVED!*
*THREE PADDED WALLS*

# OTHER FICTION AND NON-FICTION
*NANO WHAT NOW?*
Finding your editing process, revising your NaNoWriMo book and building a writing career through publishing and beyond.
*THE AUTHOR*
(award winning novella) You ever get the feeling you don't know which side of the pen you're on?

~

# WRITING AS T. W. SELLER
THEWHINESELLER.COM
*SELL THEIR STUFF*
From eBay Trading Assistants to multichannel seller assistance, your ultimate guide to consignment selling online as a part-time income or full-time business
*EBAY MARKETING MAKEOVER*
Increase sales and grow traffic to your eBay items by encouraging word of mouth, focusing on your ideal buyers, and optimizing your selling for search and mobile
*BEYOND AMAZON, EBAY, AND ETSY*
Free and low cost alternative marketplaces, shopping cart solutions and e-commerce storefronts
*THE SELLER LEDGER*
An auction organizer for selling on eBay

# ABOUT THE AUTHOR

**Hillary DePiano** is a playwright, fiction and non-fiction author best known for fantastically funny fairy tales, surprisingly sweet slapstick and unrelentingly upbeat writing advice. With over two dozen plays for everyone from pre-schoolers and up, she's honored to have had her work performed in schools and theatres around the world.

As the author of the *How to Start Writing* series, she regularly shares advice and pep as a blogger and speaker. Since 2010, Hillary heads the Northeastern New Jersey region for NaNoWriMo.org and works as a volunteer in support of their creative mission. She also writes about eBay, e-commerce, and selling online under the name T. W. Seller at TheWhineSeller.com.

For more information about her books, plays, and blogs or to connect via social media, visit HillaryDePiano.com.